# MR. PERFECT

# MR. PERFECT

by Roger Hargreaves

WORLD INTERNATIONAL
MANCHESTER

It was a perfect summer's day.

And on this perfect summer's day,
Mr Perfect was looking even more perfect
than usual.

He didn't have a hair out of place.

Mr Perfect lived in Tiptop Cottage.

And on this perfect summer's day,
his house was also looking even more
perfect than usual.

Not a curtain out of place.

I suppose you're wondering why
Tiptop Cottage was looking so perfect?

I shall tell you.

It was Mr Perfect's birthday,
and he was going to have a party.

There was a knock at the door.
"Perfect!" cried Mr Perfect.

"How very kind of you," he said, when he saw that all his guests had brought wonderful looking presents.
"Please do come in, and if no one minds, we'll open the presents later."

Nobody minded in the least.

Well almost nobody.

“WHAT’S THAT?” roared Mr Uppity.

“I don’t have any time to waste, you know!
You’d better make sure we
don’t get bored today!”

Do you think this upset Mr Perfect?

Of course not.

Mr Perfect had perfect manners,
unlike rude Mr Uppity.

“Oh no, my dear Mr Uppity,
we shan’t be bored today,” he replied.
“First of all we shall dance.”

Unfortunately, Mr Clumsy,
being his usual clumsy self,
broke a pile of plates.

Do you think this upset Mr Perfect?

Not at all!

"Don't worry, Mr Clumsy," said Mr Perfect.

And, being the perfect person he was,
and not in the least bit clumsy,
he produced a whole lot more plates ...

… made of cardboard!

Then, he brought in a cake.

It was huge.

It looked wonderful.

It smelt terrific.

And …

Mr Greedy thought it tasted delicious.

He gobbled up the whole cake
in three seconds flat!

There wasn't a crumb left for anybody else!

Do you think this upset Mr Perfect?

Not in the least.

Being perfect, he had already guessed
what would happen.

Quickly, he brought out lots of small cakes.

There were plenty for everybody.

Even Mr Perfect.

But as he was not greedy, he only ate one.

One cake was just perfect for him.

Once everything had been eaten,
Mr Perfect opened his presents.

He said as many thank-yous as
there were presents.

Well, not quite.

"What about my present?" cried Mr Mean.

Mr Mean's parcel was so small that
Mr Perfect had not seen it!

Mr Perfect opened the tiny parcel,
wrapped in newspaper.

"Oh, Mr Mean," said Mr Perfect.
"You've given me a lump of coal.
How kind of you!
It's delightful!"

"If I'd known, I'd only have given him
half a lump," grumbled Mr Mean.

“THAT’S IT! I’ve had enough!”
cried Mr Uppity, suddenly.

“I’m fed up with you, Mr Perfect. And do you know why? I’ll tell you! I have discovered that there is a most enormous, unbearable, exasperating fault with you.”

“Would you be so kind as to tell me what that might be?” asked Mr Perfect, as politely as ever.

“Don’t you understand?” cried Mr Uppity. “Your fault is ...

… that you have NO faults!”

# MR MEN question time – can you help?

## 10 sets of 4 Mr Men titles to be won!

Thank you for purchasing a Mr Men pocket book. We would be most grateful if you would help us with the answers to a few questions. Each questionnaire received will be placed in a monthly draw – you could win four Mr Men books of your choice and a free bookmark!

Is this the first Mr Men pocket book you have purchased? **Yes** ☐ **No** ☐ (please tick)

If No, how many books do you have in your collection? ____

Have you collected any Little Miss books? **Yes** ☐ **No** ☐ **How many** ____

Where do you usually shop for children's books? **Bookshop** ☐ **Newsagent** ☐ **Supermarket** ☐ **Garden Centre** ☐

Would you be interested in a presentation box to keep your Mr Men books in? **Yes** ☐ **No** ☐

Do you know that there are other types of Mr Men books? **Yes** ☐ **No** ☐

If No, would you be interested in knowing about these? **Yes** ☐ **No** ☐

Apart from Mr Men, who is your favourite children's character? ______________________

______________________________________________

## Thank you for your help.

Return this form to: Marketing Department, World International Publishing, Egmont House, PO Box111, 61 Great Ducie Street, Manchester M60 3BL.

Please tick overleaf which four Mr Men books you would like to receive if you are successful in our monthly draw and fill in your name and address details.

Signature of parent or guardian: ______________________

We may occasionally wish to advise you of other children's books that we publish. If you would rather we didn't, please tick this box ☐

Please remove this page carefully

Tick the 4 Mr Men books you would like to win.

- ☐ 1. Mr Tickle
- ☐ 2. Mr Greedy
- ☐ 3. Mr Happy
- ☐ 4. Mr Nosey
- ☐ 5. Mr Sneeze
- ☐ 6. Mr Bump
- ☐ 7. Mr Snow
- ☐ 8. Mr Messy
- ☐ 9. Mr Topsy-Turvy
- ☐ 10. Mr Silly
- ☐ 11. Mr Uppity
- ☐ 12. Mr Small
- ☐ 13. Mr Daydream
- ☐ 14. Mr Forgetful
- ☐ 15. Mr Jelly
- ☐ 16. Mr Noisy
- ☐ 17. Mr Lazy
- ☐ 18. Mr Funny
- ☐ 19. Mr Mean
- ☐ 20. Mr Chatterbox
- ☐ 21. Mr Fussy
- ☐ 22. Mr Bounce
- ☐ 23. Mr Muddle
- ☐ 24. Mr Dizzy
- ☐ 25. Mr Impossible
- ☐ 26. Mr Strong
- ☐ 27. Mr Grumpy
- ☐ 28. Mr Clumsy
- ☐ 29. Mr Quiet
- ☐ 30. Mr Rush
- ☐ 31. Mr Tall
- ☐ 32. Mr Worry
- ☐ 33. Mr Nonsense
- ☐ 34. Mr Wrong
- ☐ 35. Mr Skinny
- ☐ 36. Mr Mischief
- ☐ 37. Mr Clever
- ☐ 38. Mr Busy
- ☐ 39. Mr Slow
- ☐ 40. Mr Brave
- ☐ 41. Mr Grumble
- ☐ 42. Mr Perfect
- ☐ 43. Mr Cheerful

Your name ______________________________

Address ______________________________

______________________________

______________________________ Postcode ______________

# SPECIAL OFFERS FOR MR MEN AND LITTLE MISS READERS

In every Mr Men and Little Miss book you will find a special token. Collect only six tokens and we will send you a super poster of your choice featuring all your favourite Mr Men or Little Miss friends.

And for the first 4,000 readers we hear from, we will send you a Mr Men activity pad* and a bookmark* as well – absolutely free!

**Return this page with six tokens from Mr Men and/or Little Miss books to:**
Marketing Department, World International Publishing, Egmont House, PO Box 111, 61 Great Ducie Street, Manchester M60 3BL.

Your name: ____________________

Address: ____________________

____________________

____________________ Postcode: ____________________

Signature of parent or guardian: ____________________

I enclose **six** tokens – please send me a Mr Men poster ☐

I enclose **six** tokens – please send me a Little Miss poster ☐

We may occasionally wish to advise you of other children's books that we publish. If you would rather we didn't, please tick this box ☐

**while stocks last*

*(Please note: this offer is limited to a maximum of two posters per household.)*

Collect six of these tokens. You will find one inside every Mr Men and Little Miss book which has this special offer.

**1 TOKEN**

Please remove this page carefully

# MR MEN question time – can you help?

Thank you for purchasing this Mr Men or Little Miss pocket book. We would be most grateful if you would help us with the answers to a few questions.

Would you be interested in a presentation box to keep your Mr Men or Little Miss books in? **Yes** ☐ **No** ☐ (please tick)

Apart from Mr Men or Little Miss, who is your favourite children's character? ______________________

If you could write a Mr Men and a Little Miss book, what names would you give your characters? **Mr** ______________________

**Little Miss** ______________________

If applicable, where did you buy this book from?
Please give the stockist's name and address.

Name: ______________________

Address: ______________________

______________________

______________________

**THANK YOU FOR YOUR HELP**